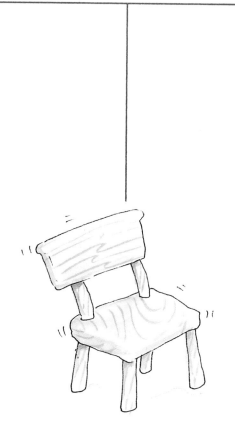

# Millie and Bombassa

**Make friends with the
funniest duo in town!**

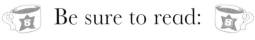 Be sure to read:
*Cash Crazy!*

... and lots, lots more!

# Dizzy D.I.Y.!

written and illustrated by
## Shoo Rayner

**SCHOLASTIC**

Scholastic Children's Books,
Commonwealth House, 1-19 New Oxford Street,
London, WC1A 1NU, UK
a division of Scholastic Ltd
London ~ New York ~ Toronto ~ Sydney ~ Auckland
Mexico City ~ New Delhi ~ Hong Kong

First published by Scholastic Ltd, 2002

ISBN 0 439 99466 7

Printed and bound by Oriental Press, Dubai, UAE

10 9 8 7 6 5 4 3 2 1

# Chapter One

Bombassa was doing his favourite thing …
sleeping. And he was dreaming about
doing his second favourite thing … dunking
biscuits in his tea.

He dreamed he was drinking and dunking in a beautiful garden, where it was nice and warm, the sun was shining and someone was ringing a bell…

Tinkle-tinkle, Ring-ring

Someone was ringing a bell? That wasn't supposed to happen in his dream.

The bell was very loud.

It rang on and on…

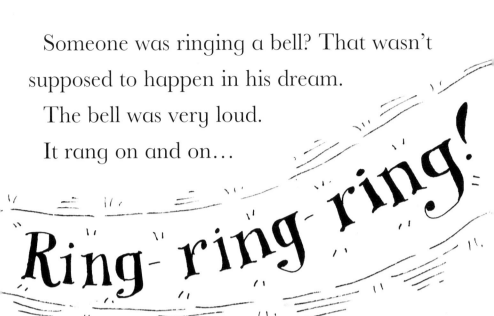

*Ring - ring - ring!*

Then something tickled Bombassa's ears. Suddenly, his lovely dream wasn't very lovely any more.

"Wake up!" said a small voice.

Bombassa groaned. "I don't want to wake up."

"Wake up!" said the little voice again. "It's your Auntie Daz on the phone."

Bombassa opened one eye. His best friend Millie was flapping her wings and hopping about on the end of his nose.

"Come on!" said Millie. "Auntie Daz wants to speak to you."

Just then Auntie Daz's impatient voice screeched out of the earpiece.

Bombassa fell out of bed, and stumbled into the sitting room.

He sat down on his wobbly chair
and picked up the phone.

"Hello, Auntie
Daz," he yawned.

"Bombassa!" squawked Auntie Daz. "I
suppose you've just woken up, have you?"
Auntie Daz thought Bombassa
was the laziest person
in the world.

Bombassa looked at the time. It was nearly eleven o'clock!

He wriggled about on the chair while he tried to think of an excuse. The chair creaked and groaned and wobbled and suddenly an idea popped into his head.

"No, no, I've been awake for hours Auntie," he lied! "I've been doing a bit of DIY… fixing my wobbly chair."

"Oh!" said a surprised Auntie Daz. "Well I'll look forward to seeing that. I'm coming to town today, so I'll pop in and see you for tea at four o'clock. That should give you plenty of time to buy a cake. Bye!"

She hung up before Bombassa had the chance to reply.

# Chapter Two

Bombassa was wide awake now. He looked around him. His house was very untidy … as usual.

"What are we going to do?" he asked Millie. "Auntie Daz is coming for tea and I told her that I've fixed my wobbly chair!"

"Action stations!" said Millie. "We'll have a cup of tea and then we can think about the chair."

Millie knew that Bombassa would be no use at all until he'd had a cup of tea.

While the kettle boiled,
Bombassa started
sorting through
a pile of books.

"Oh look!" said Bombassa. "Here's that
book I got about the Japanese Tea
Ceremony. They take tea very seriously in
Japan, you know."

"No one takes tea more seriously than
you!" laughed Millie.

The Japanese
Tea Ceremony

When the tea was made, Bombassa sat down on the wobbly chair. He dunked two huge biscuits in his huge cup of tea and looked at the book.

The book showed people sitting down at very low tables drinking tea from bowls.

In the middle of the book there was a big picture of a Japanese Tea Garden.

Bombassa sighed. "It looks just like the garden in my lovely dream."

"Come along!" chirped Millie. "There's no time for daydreaming. You've got to get that chair fixed before Auntie Daz arrives."

# Chapter Three

Bombassa fetched his tool kit. He measured the chair legs and wrote down how long each one was.

"You see," he explained to Millie. "This leg is longer than the others. I need to cut off one centimetre, then they'll all be the same."

"Are you sure it was that leg?" asked
Millie. "Remember, the secret of DIY is
to measure twice and cut once."

Bombassa measured
the legs again to be sure.

"Yes, definitely," said Bombassa. "I just
need to cut a bit off this one."

He carefully sawed one centimetre off the
leg, and turned the chair the right way up.

Then he sat on the
chair to test it.

It still wobbled.
In fact it wobbled
even worse
than before!

Bombassa measured the legs again.

"I don't understand it!" he exclaimed.
"I must have cut the wrong leg.
Now I'll have to cut bits
off the other legs to
make them all the same!"

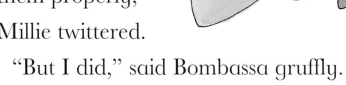

"You can't
have measured
them properly,"
Millie twittered.

"But I did," said Bombassa gruffly.
"You watched me."

He cut some more off the legs, but the
chair still wobbled.

"You won't have anything
left to sit on soon!" said
Millie. "Give me the
tape measure."

Bombassa folded
his arms and watched
Millie carefully
measure each
leg.

"If you cut where I've marked," she explained, "all the legs will be equal."

Bombassa sawed the legs again and turned the chair over. He sat on it and smiled. "Hooray! It doesn't wobble any more!"

"Hey!" he said, as he reached for his cup of tea. "What happened to the table? It's too high!"

Millie looked down at Bombassa. "The table's not too high," she muttered. "Your chair is too low!"

Bombassa rolled his eyes. "That means I'll have to lower the table!"

He measured the table legs and cut them shorter, but now the table was wobbly!

Millie tapped her foot, impatiently. "Shall I do the measuring?" she asked.

Soon, she had measured the legs properly and Bombassa had sawn them so that they were all equal. But now the chair was too high!

Once again,
Millie carefully
measured the chair

and Bombassa
cut some more
off the legs.

"At last!" said Bombassa. "No more
wobbling and
the table is just
the right
height."

"But you can't ask Auntie Daz to sit on that!" said Millie, pointing at the chair. "You might as well ask her to sit on the floor."

Millie was right. The chair and the table no longer had legs … they had stumps!

# Chapter Four

Bombassa looked worried. "What are we going to do? What will Auntie Daz say? Look at the time. Auntie Daz will be here in half an hour. I'm supposed to have bought a cake! All we've got is broken biscuits. Auntie Daz will be so cross with me. She'll think I've been in bed all day."

Bombassa slumped down on the little chair and felt like crying. He picked up the Japanese Tea Ceremony book and gazed at the picture of the tea garden.

"If only I hadn't woken up this morning," he thought out loud. "If only I could have stayed in my lovely dream."

"Wait a minute," said Millie. "Look! Your table looks just like a Japanese tea-table now. You could treat Auntie Daz to a Japanese Tea Ceremony. I'm sure they don't have cake in a Japanese Tea Ceremony!"

Bombassa picked Millie up and squeezed her tight. "You're a genius!" he said. "Put the kettle on, there's no time to lose."

They set to work, trying to make the
room look like the pictures in the book.

They covered the table with a cloth and
put a cushion on the chair and some more
cushions on the floor.

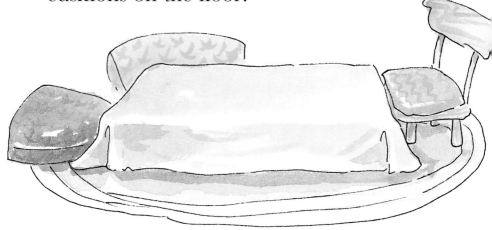

With a few flowerpots and a twiggy stick,
Bombassa made a little
indoor garden.

Millie picked a flower and placed it in a vase on the table.

Next Bombassa covered the clothes airer with a blanket and hung up a paper lantern that he found in the back of a cupboard.

Finally, they folded some paper into origami dishes and put them on the table.

When Auntie Daz rang the doorbell,
everything was ready. Bombassa answered
the door wearing his silk dressing gown.
He held his hands together and bowed.
"Welcome, honourable Auntie."

# Chapter Five

Auntie Daz took one look at Bombassa's
dressing gown and tut-tutted loudly.
"That's just typical," she snorted. "You've
been in bed all day, haven't you?"

Bombassa smiled again and bowed even
lower. "Follow me, Auntie."

Bombassa pulled out the chair to let
Auntie Daz sit down.
"What is going on?"
she asked.

Millie and Bombassa smiled at each other. "Welcome to our Japanese tea-room," they said, together.

Auntie Daz sank very slowly on to the chair. She looked most uncomfortable.

Bombassa carefully tore open three tea bags and emptied them into the teapot.

Then he filled it with hot water and put on the lid.

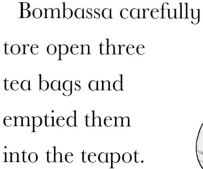

He turned the teapot round three times, tapped it twice, and poured a cup for Auntie Daz.

"What are you doing?" Auntie Daz asked impatiently. "The tea will be swimming with tea leaves!"

"Just so!" said Bombassa, mysteriously.

Bombassa bowed and smiled. He held the biscuit tin as if it were a treasure chest. He made strange signs over the tin before he opened it.

He took out some biscuits and arranged
them in the paper dishes.

"What?!" boomed Auntie Daz. "No cake?"

"Shhh!" Millie whispered. "Bombassa is
preparing the Japanese Biscuit Dunking
Ceremony. It's very serious."

Millie and Bombassa dunked the biscuits in their tea and munched them in silence. Auntie Daz didn't want to be left out, so she did the same.

When they were
finished, Bombassa
stood up, bowed
and walked to
the front door.

Auntie Daz turned to Millie. "What's
happening now?" she asked.

"The ceremony is over," Millie whispered.

"Oh!" said Auntie Daz. She looked at her watch. "I'd better be going then."

She struggled to get up from the little chair.

"Well," she puffed. "That was very interesting. What a thoughtful boy you are, doing the Japanese Biscuit Dunking Ceremony, just for me."

Bombassa stood by the door, smiling and bowing. "We must do it again, honourable Auntie."

Auntie Daz rubbed her aching back and winced as she kissed him goodbye. "Maybe you could dream up something different next time … something that uses proper chairs and tables?"

Bombassa waved goodbye as Auntie Daz limped down the path.

Then he closed the
door and marched
off to his bedroom.

"Where are you
going?" asked Millie.

"Bed!" he boomed. "Auntie Daz made
me promise that I'd dream up something
different for the next time she comes to tea.
I'm going to start right now!"

As he pulled the duvet over his head,
he added, "...and switch the phone off...
I don't want to be disturbed!"